PUFFIN BOOKS

The Brain-Blasting Adventures
of Norman Thorman

Lorna Kent was born in London and moved to Brighton
to study illustration, where her tutor was Raymond
Briggs. She now works from a busy studio near the sea-
front. Humour plays a large and important part in all
her works. She has now written four books featuring
Norman Thorman.

The Brain-Blasting
Adventures of
Norman Thorman

Lorna Kent

PUFFIN BOOKS

PUFFIN BOOKS

Published by the Penguin Group
Penguin Books Ltd, 27 Wrights Lane, London W8 5TZ, England
Penguin Books USA Inc., 375 Hudson Street, New York, New York 10014, USA
Penguin Books Australia Ltd, Ringwood, Victoria, Australia
Penguin Books Canada Ltd, 10 Alcorn Avenue, Toronto, Ontario, Canada M4V 3B2
Penguin Books (NZ) Ltd, 182–190 Wairau Road, Auckland 10, New Zealand

Penguin Books Ltd, Registered Offices: Harmondsworth, Middlesex, England

Norman Thorman and the Towering Tarantula of Torremolinos
first published by Hamish Hamilton Ltd 1993
Norman Thorman and the Mystery of the Missing Mummy
first published by Hamish Hamilton Ltd 1994
This omnibus edition published in Puffin Books 1995
1 3 5 7 9 10 8 6 4 2

Text and illustrations copyright © Lorna Kent 1993, 1994
All rights reserved

The moral right of the author/illustrator has been asserted

Made and printed in Great Britain by Clays Ltd, St Ives plc

Contents

For my mother

Chapter One

Schoolboy Norman Thorman was on his way home from the trip of a lifetime. He had spent the whole of the school holidays staying with his uncle and aunt in the Spanish seaside resort of Torremolinos. Norman sat back in his aeroplane seat and thought about all the adventures they had had together. But little did he know that the biggest adventure was about to begin.

It all started when he got back home. As he unpacked his bag, a tiny spider that had been hiding in a rolled-up sock decided to make its escape.

"You're a long way from home," said Norman, picking it up gently. "I'm afraid you'll have to live with me now."

The spider ran around Norman's palm for a few moments and then disappeared up his sleeve.

"Hey, come back!" cried Norman. He felt the spider run across his chest, over his shoulder and down his back. "Stop it, you're tickling me," he laughed.

As Norman thrashed about trying to catch his new pet, he lost his balance and crashed into his desk. He ended up on the floor covered in the chemistry experiment he had set up before the holidays.

"Oh no!" groaned Norman. "That's the end of my miracle hair restorer experiment. Only one more week and it would have been ready."

He rescued the spider from a pool of liquid, popped it into his bug bottle and wrote ARACHNID on the label.

"I think I'll call you Tarquin," said Norman as he hid the bug bottle under his bed. "We can't have Mum and Dad finding you. They don't like spiders."

That night Norman tossed and turned and had some really strange dreams. The next morning he ate his breakfast in a daze.

"Oh Norman, you're not even dressed yet," snapped Mrs Thorman. "And what's the matter with your hair? What have you done to it?"

"Nothing," yawned Norman as he wandered off to get ready for school.

"Well, it's too late to do anything with it now," flapped Mrs Thorman. "Honestly, Norman, sometimes I'd swear your hair grows inches overnight. I think we'll take a trip to the hairdresser's after school."

Chapter Two

The first lesson that morning was
football.

"What's the matter with your hair,
boy!" bellowed Mr Fitt, the games
teacher. "Why is it sticking up in the
air like that?"

"I don't know, sir," replied
Norman, reaching up to feel his hair.
It certainly didn't feel normal. It felt
as if he'd washed it in glue, which

of course he hadn't.

"You surprise me, Norman!" sighed Mr Fitt. "You should pay more attention to your appearance, especially as you are the Register Monitor."

"I didn't do it on purpose," explained Norman, but Mr Fitt wasn't listening.

As Norman changed into his football kit he kept trying to flatten his hair down, but it was no use. The harder he tried the stiffer and spikier it became. All Norman's friends were amazed. They thought it was a brilliant hairstyle. That was until it got so spiky it burst three footballs and Norman was sent off.

"Whatever it is you've put on your

hair, I want it washed off immediately!" demanded Mr Fitt.

Norman washed his hair but it made no difference. He began to think it was one of his dad's practical jokes. "He could have put glue in the shampoo bottle . . . No, even Dad wouldn't do that."

Norman sat in the changing room waiting for the game to finish. He was so busy reading his book that he didn't notice what was happening to his hair. Slowly it grew about six inches, pointing straight up in the air. Then the whole lot began to twist into a stiff peak on top of his head.

After Norman heard the final whistle he ran outside to see what

the score was.

When Mr Fitt saw Norman's hair
he was so shocked, he walked
straight into the goal post and almost
knocked himself out!

"What the? . . . How? . . .
Why? . . . " he gasped. "I shall be
writing to your parents for an
explanation!"

At lunch Norman was really fed up. What was causing his hair to behave so strangely?

"At least things can't get any worse," he thought. But they did . . . The dreaded hair jokes started.

"Where does Norman Thorman live?"

"In a block of PLAITS!"

"What's Norman Thorman's favourite way of travelling?"

"By HAIROPLANE!"

"What does Norman Thorman eat at tea time?"

"Currant BUNS!"

Norman was relieved when school was over. As soon as the bell went he dashed off to meet his mum at the school gate.

"Good grief!" shrieked Mrs Thorman when she saw Norman's hair. "You look like a unicorn!"

"Come on, Mum," said Norman, pulling his stunned mother through the school gates. "Let's go and get my hair cut before I hear any more corny jokes."

At Baldycoot's Unisex Hair Salon, the hairdresser shook her head. "There's something very wrong here," she said, inspecting her bent and twisted scissors. "Norman's hair is so strong I can't cut it!"

"That does it!" exclaimed Mrs Thorman. "I'm taking you straight to the hospital."

The Thorman's were well known at the hospital, as this wasn't the first time that something weird had happened to Norman.

"Hello, Norman," said the doctor. "And how do you feel today?"

"I feel stupid," muttered Norman.

"He's a little sensitive at the moment," explained Mrs Thorman. "He's had a bad day at school."

Mrs Thorman whisked the paper bag off Norman's head. "What do you think, Doctor?" she asked.

"Well I never!" exclaimed the doctor, staring at Norman's hair. "You really are full of surprises."

"I suppose this means lots of tests," said Mrs Thorman.

"I'm afraid it does," replied the doctor. "But don't worry, I don't think it's serious."

"Huh, that's easy for you to say," said Norman. "How can I be a Register Monitor with hair like this?"

Mrs Thorman left Norman with the doctor and went off to phone her husband at work. "This is not going to be easy to explain," she thought.

That evening Mr and Mrs Thorman sat in the hospital waiting room while Norman was being examined. Mrs Thorman wondered if the new brand of shampoo she'd bought recently could be responsible for Norman's condition.

Norman and the doctor eventually emerged.

"Well, apart from his hair growing in a most unusual manner, your son appears to be in perfect health," said the doctor. "We shall be sending samples to a specialist for further investigation. And don't worry, we'll soon get to the ROOT of the problem."

"Oh no!" thought Norman. "Not *more* hair jokes."

It was quite dark when the Thormans got home. Norman was the first to notice something was very wrong.

"What's my bed doing on the front lawn?" he gasped.

"What on earth? . . . " began Mr Thorman.

"Look!" screamed Mrs Thorman, pointing up to the huge hole in the side of the house.

"That's my bedroom!" shrieked Norman.

"I just knew that chemistry set would lead to trouble," cried Mrs Thorman.

"Oh Norman, you really are the limit," snapped Mr Thorman.

Norman began to protest. "But

I haven't . . . It wasn't . . . I
didn't . . . " But it was useless. Mr
Thorman was busy trying to cover
the hole with plastic sheeting while
Mrs Thorman phoned the builder.

As Norman picked up the rest of
his belongings that were scattered on
the lawn he saw his bug bottle in
pieces on the path. "Poor little
Tarquin, he didn't stand a chance."

Chapter Three

Norman spent a comfortable night
on the sofa and woke feeling
refreshed. He jumped out of bed and
ran into the kitchen for breakfast.
The look of astonishment on his
mum and dad's face soon reminded
him of his problem. His hair had
grown even longer and was sticking
out of his head in big spikes.

"Stop looking at me like that,"

snapped Norman, feeling his head. "I can't help it."

"I'm sorry, son," grinned Mr Thorman. "It's just that you remind me of someone . . . something . . . "

"George!" warned Mrs Thorman.

"I know what it is!" laughed Mr Thorman. "You look like the Statue of Liberty!"

Even Mrs Thorman began to laugh. "Don't mind us," she smiled.

"It's just that we're not used to seeing you like this."

Norman groaned. "Try not to worry, darling," said Mrs Thorman. "I'm sure you'll be back to normal soon."

"Yes," said Mr Thorman. "As the old saying goes: HAIR today, gone tomorrow!"

"It's not funny!" shouted Norman. "I don't know what it's going to do next!"

After lunch Mr Thorman hid himself behind a large newspaper. This was partly because he was interested in the news and partly to stop himself laughing at Norman's hair.

"Good grief!" cried Mr Thorman,

suddenly sitting bolt upright. "How extraordinary!" he exclaimed, pointing to the newspaper.

"Town in Towering Tarantula Terror! . . . Traffic was brought to a standstill today as a giant tarantula, with a body the size of a very large elephant, made its way through the town towards the shopping centre. A government spokesman who was at the scene said . . . 'We do not yet know how the tarantula came to be in this country or why it has grown to such an enormous size. We have a theory that a strange chemical reaction has taken place and we have a team of top government scientists working on it at this very moment. The public are strongly urged to stay at home until we have the creature under control.'"

"Well I suppose it had to happen one day, what with all that chemical rubbish they spray on the fields these days," sighed Mr Thorman. "At least nobody interferes with our vegetable plot."

"They did once," said Norman, remembering an incident involving marrows. But that's another story.

Suddenly there was an urgent knock at the door. "Oh no!" gasped Norman as he rushed upstairs to his bedroom. "I don't want anyone to see me like this."

"Hello, I'm from Mars," said the man on the doorstep.

"Yes and I'm the Queen of

England," replied Mr Thorman, quickly closing the door.

"Who was it, dear?" asked Mrs Thorman.

"Oh, just a mad man who claims he's from Mars," replied Mr Thorman.

"Poor chap should be in a hospital," said Mrs Thorman.

"Hello . . . hello," called the voice through the letterbox. "I'm Professor Fly from M.A.R.S. The Mutant Arachnid Recovery Service. I must speak to your son Norman!"

"Oh no," groaned an embarrassed Mr Thorman as he rushed to open the door. "I'm sorry about that," he apologized. "I thought you were a bit umm . . . err . . . Do come in."

"Would you like a cup of tea?"
asked Mrs Thorman.

"I'm afraid there's no time for
tea," explained Professor Fly. "The
hospital has informed me that
Norman's tests reveal a strange
unknown chemical also present in
the hairs from a gigantic tarantula!"

Norman had been sitting at the
top of the stairs and had heard
everything. He thought about the
spider he had accidently brought
back from Torremolinos, the

chemistry experiment, his weird hair, the huge hole in his bedroom wall and the broken bug bottle on the path. Suddenly everything became clear.

"Oh no!" he gasped. "The giant tarantula must be Tarquin! He probably ate some of my experimental hair restorer when it fell on us. That would also explain why my hair is behaving so strangely. Tarquin must have crashed through my bedroom wall when he grew too big!"

Suddenly a local news flash appeared on the television. Norman could just see it from the top of the stairs.

"At this very moment the town

centre is being held in a vice-like grip
of terror. A terrifying giant tarantula
is towering over the shopping centre.
The creature has doubled in size
since it was discovered in the early
hours of this morning and is
continuing to grow rapidly." The
camera zoomed in for a close up shot
of the tarantula.

"It *is* Tarquin!" thought Norman.
"I recognize him!"

The newsflash continued . . . "The
emergency services are at the scene,
but surely it's only a matter of time
before something dreadful happens.
This is Roger Roving reporting for
Channel Four."

"It's not Tarquin's fault," thought
Norman. "He doesn't want to hurt

anyone. He may be huge but he's still only a baby."

Norman felt terrible. "It's all my fault," he said. "I've got do something!"

He wasn't sure what he could do but he knew he had to act fast! He ran into his bedroom and locked the door behind him. Then he grabbed his chemistry set, opened the window and climbed down the drainpipe.

"I hope Mum and Dad don't notice I've gone for a while," thought Norman as he jumped on his bike and sped off towards the shopping centre.

Chapter Four

When Norman reached the town centre it was chaos. He soon spotted who was in charge of the situation. It was a large man with a loud voice wearing an army uniform covered in stripes and medals. Norman took his Register Monitor's badge from his pocket and pinned it to his jumper before introducing himself.

"Norman Thorman reporting for

duty, sir!" saluted Norman.

General Boom was not easily shocked but the sight of Norman's spiky, helmet-like hair left him speechless for a few seconds.

Norman explained all about Tarquin and the failed hair restorer experiment. "He doesn't want to hurt anyone," he said. "He's only a baby really."

"He may not want to hurt anyone," said General Boom, "but it's extremely inconvenient for him to be sitting in the middle of the shopping centre. There are a lot of people who don't take kindly to spiders."

"You can say that again!" said an irate shopkeeper. "Nobody can get in or out of my shop with that great big lump sitting in the way!"

"He's not a lump," protested Norman. "He's a tarantula. And he's just as upset as everyone else."

"The situation has become critical, Norman," explained the General. "The tarantula has now become so big, it's stuck between Macdougal's hamburger restaurant and Woolco's supermarket. If it gets any bigger or if it tries to move it will knock the buildings down."

"I've got to do something now or it will be too late," thought Norman.

Norman waited until General Boom was busy giving orders, then he tucked his chemistry set up his jumper and ran towards

Macdougal's, jumping over bags of shopping that had been dropped in the panic. Eventually he entered the back door of Macdougal's and found himself in the kitchen. When he saw all the hamburgers he had a brainwave. Without a moments hesitation he piled them all onto a big tray and took the lift to the top floor. When he was about half way up, the lift began to shake. "Oh no!" thought Norman. "Tarquin's getting restless, I must hurry!"

The lift doors opened and Norman bounded up the last few stairs and out onto the roof.

Suddenly he was face to face with Tarquin, whose big, sad eyes were filled with confusion.

"Don't worry, Tarquin!" called Norman. "I got you into this mess and now I'm going to get you out!"

Then Norman whipped out his chemistry set and started to mix up all kinds of chemical concoctions. One by one he smeared the hamburgers with the different experimental antidotes.

"I'm sorry I have to experiment on you," said Norman. "But this is an emergency."

Tarquin was very hungry and soon wolfed his way through most of the hamburgers. Unfortunately nothing seemed to be working.

"Only one hamburger left," sighed Norman. "This is our last chance."

Just then Norman's concentration was shattered by the screeching of car brakes down below. Three people jumped out of the car and ran towards Macdougal's.

"Norman! Norman!" shouted the woman. "Come down from that building at once!"

"I'm coming up to get you, Norman," shouted the man. "Stay away from the edge!"

"Oh no!" gasped Norman, recognising the voices. "It's Mum and Dad with Professor Fly. I need more time to mix the last potion."

Norman furiously mixed the last of the chemicals together and spread them on the last burger. Tarquin swallowed it in one gulp as Norman sank to the floor exhausted. "I'm sorry, Tarquin," he sighed. "There's nothing more I can do now."

After about a minute Norman noticed a strange look in Tarquin's eyes. Gradually the creature began to shrink. Slowly at first and then quite quickly. "I've done it! I've done it!" shrieked Norman, jumping up and down. "I've discovered the antidote."

In only ten minutes Tarquin had shrunk to his original size. Professor Fly quickly put him in his super-secure unbreakable bug box.

Everyone cheered and clapped as Norman hugged his parents. "Well done, Norman!" boomed General Boom. "If you want a career in the army you've only got to ask, I'm sure something could be done about that hair."

"Thank you," replied Norman.
"But I've already got a very
important job as a Register
Monitor."

"You're a genius, Norman!"
beamed Professor Fly. "How did you
work out the antidote formula so
quickly?"

"In my job I'm expected to know
a lot of things," said Norman,
proudly polishing his Register
Monitor's badge on his sleeve.

Fortunately Mr and Mrs Thorman
were so thankful that Norman was
safe they forgot to tell him off, which
was a relief for Norman.

"What will happen to Tarquin
now?" asked Norman.

"We'll keep him under observation
at MARS for a while," replied
Professor Fly. "Just to make sure he
doesn't start growing again. Then we
will send him back home."

Norman was quite sad to say goodbye to Tarquin, but he knew it was for the best.

The antidote took a little longer to work on Norman. It wasn't until later that evening at dinner, that his hair collapsed into his soup.

"We could have been rich if my miracle hair restorer experiment had worked," Norman told his parents. "Maybe with a bit more work I could . . ."

"I think you've done quite enough experimenting, dear," said Mrs Thorman.

"Never mind," said Mr Thorman. "You may not be the inventor of a miracle hair restorer, but there's one thing you'll always be."

"What's that?" asked Norman, expecting the worst.

"Our HAIRO."

And, of course, everyone groaned.

Norman Thorman and the Mystery
of the Missing Mummy

For my brother Keith Kent

Chapter One

For schoolboy Norman Thorman it
was turning out to be one of the most
interesting days he had ever had.
Norman's teacher, Miss Mindbenda,
had taken the class to the Relic
Museum to see a very special
exhibition on the ancient Egyptians.
Norman could hardly believe his eyes
as he stared up at a real ancient
Egyptian mummy. "Wow! that's
amazing," he gasped. But little
did he know just how amazing it

was going to get.

Norman's jaw dropped open as he listened to Sir Gadabout Binthere-Dunnit, the famous explorer, describe how he found the dark airless tomb where the mummy and all its belongings had lain undisturbed for thousands of years. Everyone thought the mummy was really spooky, and the thunderstorm that was raging outside certainly added to the atmosphere.

Norman had just finished writing SARCOPHAGUS on his drawing of the mummy's coffin, when something extraordinary happened. A large branch from an overhanging tree outside snapped off in the storm. It crashed through a skylight, narrowly

missing Sir Gadabout, and smashed
the display case. A small, carved
wooden egg rolled towards Norman
and stopped at his feet. As he picked
it up a small puff of dust shot out of
the egg and went straight up his
nose. Suddenly Norman gave one
almighty sneeze!

"Norman! Are you all right?"
asked Miss Mindbenda.

But Norman didn't answer. His
eyes glazed over and he stared
blindly into the distance.

"He's gone into a trance, Miss,"
pointed out one of Norman's
classmates. "Look, his eyes have
gone all funny."

"I bet that mummy's got a curse
on it!" gasped another.

"CURSE OF THE MUMMY!
CURSE OF THE MUMMY!"
chanted the class.

"They may be right," said Sir
Gadabout, looking worried. "When I
first discovered the mummy it was
clutching that egg like a treasured
possession. I said it was a mistake to
separate them."

"There's an inscription on that
egg in hieroglyphics," said Miss

Mindbenda. "What does it say?"

The colour drained from Sir Gadabout's face as he translated the ancient pictures and symbols. "It says, 'KNOW ME, KNOW MY MUMMY'," he gulped.

"What a lot of superstitious twaddle," huffed Miss Mindbenda.

Suddenly Norman began to speak in a very strange language.

"Plunderin' pyramids!" exclaimed Sir Gadabout. "The boy's speaking ancient Egyptian!"

"He can't be," replied Miss Mindbenda. "He's only just started to learn French!"

Miss Mindbenda took Norman straight to hospital, where he was well known for his unusual medical

history. He had to take a lot of tests but eventually the doctor told him, "You've got nothing more than an unexplainable language hiccup."

Norman frowned. "Just because it doesn't hurt doesn't mean it isn't awful," he groaned. "How can I be a proper Register Monitor with a language hiccup?"

But of course the doctor couldn't
understand what he was saying.

That evening Norman's parents
visited him in hospital.

"He can understand and read
English," the doctor told them. "But
I'm afraid, at the moment, he can
only speak ancient Egyptian."

"Can he write at all?" asked Mrs
Thorman.

"Hieroglyphics," replied the doctor.

"Bless you!" said Mr Thorman, passing the tissues.

"This is no time for jokes, George!" scolded Mrs Thorman.

"I'm afraid we don't know how long it will last," said the doctor. "It's the first case of its kind. We'll keep Norman under observation tonight and you can take him home tomorrow."

Norman was fed up. He kept forgetting he had a language hiccup. He tried to tell his parents all the amazing things that had happened to him that day, but the blank look on their faces reminded him that they couldn't understand a word he said.

Norman's frustration was interrupted by the nurse helping a new patient into the next bed. "This is Professor Lip," she said. "You will have someone to talk to, Norman. Professor Lip is a silly!"

"How rude!" exclaimed Mr Thorman. He turned to Professor Lip, who was bandaged from head to toe. "I'm sure you're not the least bit silly."

"Let me explain," smiled Professor Lip, offering a heavily bandaged hand to shake. "I am a S.I.L.A.E. It stands for Specialist in Languages of Ancient Egypt."

"Oh, I see!" blushed Mr Thorman. Norman stifled a laugh under the bedcovers. This was one situation he would not allow his dad to forget.

Professor Lip noticed Mrs Thorman looking anxiously at his bandages. "It's not catching, or painful," he explained. "I've got an allergy to biological washing powder. It itches like mad but the doctor told me it will be gone in a couple of days."

When visiting time was over, Norman's parents left him talking excitedly to Professor Lip.

Norman told him every single thing that had happened that day.

"Slow down, slow down," laughed Professor Lip. "I may be a S.I.L.A.E. but I can hardly keep up with you."

"I just know there's something really strange about that egg," said Norman. "I don't know what it is yet, but I've got a feeling I'll soon find out."

Chapter Two

Gradually Norman's eyelids grew heavy and he fell into a deep sleep.

In the middle of the night, as Norman dreamed of pyramids and mummies, Professor Lip felt so itchy he couldn't get to sleep. He eventually gave up trying and went for a walk.

A little while later Norman slowly became aware of a shadowy bandaged figure at the foot of his bed. "Norman . . . Norman," it called. "Where is the egg, Norman? Where is the egg?"

Norman was so drowsy he wasn't sure if he was dreaming or not.

"Come on now, Professor," said the night nurse, grabbing the bandaged figure by the arm. "Get back into bed. I'm sure Norman's heard enough ancient Egyptian for one night."

"Norman . . . Where is the egg? . . . The egg . . ."

"It's no good talking that mumbo jumbo to me," scolded the nurse. "And look at the state of those bandages; they're filthy. You look as if you'd been dragged through a hedge backwards." She tucked in the sheets really tight and went back to her office.

When Norman woke the next morning he noticed Professor Lip's bandages were spotless. "It must have been a dream," he said to himself.

It wasn't long before Norman's parents came to take him home. They all said goodbye to Professor Lip, who was just nodding off.

"We may need to borrow you as a translator if Norman doesn't get back to normal soon," called Mrs Thorman.

When Norman returned to school the following day, he was relieved to find he still had his old job.

"I see no reason why Norman's

language hiccup should interfere with his duties as Register Monitor," Miss Mindbenda told the class.

The rest of the morning went quite smoothly. In Art, he painted a picture of a pyramid with a glorious red sunset in the background. Miss Mindbenda put it on the wall. In English he wrote a whole story in hieroglyphics.

At playtime everyone crowded around Norman, asking questions and wanting him to say something in ancient Egyptian.

"Can you write my name in hieroglyphics?"

"How do you add up in ancient Egyptian?"

This was fine for a while, but, as

Norman suspected, the jokes soon started.

"Is your MUMMY coming to collect you from school, Norman?"

"What kind of music does Norman like? . . . WRAP!"

"What did Norman have for his lunch? . . . A cheese SCROLL!"

"What type of paper does Norman like to write on? . . . SANDPAPER!"

By the end of the day Norman was looking forward to going home.

"I just hope Dad doesn't start with his corny jokes when I get back," he sighed.

Chapter Three

When Norman got home his mum
had made an enormous chocolate
cake to cheer him up. After dinner,
Mrs Thorman was just about to get
the cake from the kitchen, when the
doctor phoned from the hospital.

"We found nothing unusual about
the dust in the egg," he told Mrs
Thorman. "I've returned it to the
museum. How is Norman today?"

"He's a little fed up with being
teased at school," replied Mrs

Thorman. "But you know what children are like!" she said, glaring at her husband. Mr Thorman hid behind his newspaper and regretted his joke about Norman being a Mummy's boy. But everyone soon forgot the bad joke when he suddenly started to read excitedly from the paper.

"Listen to this!" he exclaimed. "'MUSEUM MUMMY MYSTERIOUSLY MISSING. An ancient Egyptian mummy on loan from the Egyptian government has been stolen from the Relic Museum. The police are not taking seriously reports that it is alive and running around the town. Shaken pensioner, 83-year-old Mrs Violet Boiledsweet told the police: "It poked its head through my kitchen window. I clobbered it with a packet of frozen fish fingers and it ran off!"'"

"Alive indeed!" laughed Mr Thorman. "It's obviously someone dressed up playing a silly joke on everyone."

"Some people watch far too much

television," added Mrs Thorman.

When Norman saw the newspaper photograph of the stolen mummy he suddenly realised he had seen it not once but TWICE before. The first time was at the museum and the second time at the hospital.

"It wasn't a dream after all!" he shouted, jumping up and down with excitement. "The mummy is alive! It was at the hospital and the nurse thought it was Professor Lip and put it to bed. It's looking for the egg and it thinks I've got it!"

Of course, Norman's parents couldn't understand a word he was saying.

"Calm down, Norman!" said Mr Thorman. "You're over-excited and that's not good for you in your condition."

Norman was sent to bed, protesting in ancient Egyptian.

A little later there was an urgent knock at the door.

"I'm Sir Gadabout Binthere-Dunnit," said Sir Gadabout, shaking Mr Thorman's hand. "I've lost my mummy."

"Well, you're old enough to look after yourself!" smiled Mr Thorman.

"This is no time for jokes," snapped Sir Gadabout. "I'm mad!"

"Ahh, don't tell me," smirked Mr Thoman. "That's got to stand for something like . . . Mummies in Ancient Dynasties?"

"No!" replied Sir Gadabout. "I

mean I'm hopping mad! The entire
Egyptian government is hopping
mad. They want me to pack up the
whole exhibition and ship it back to
Egypt tomorrow morning. If that
mummy isn't back in its box by then,
there's going to be a serious
diplomatic incident."

"I'm afraid it isn't here," said Mr
Thorman.

"I was hoping Norman might have
some information that could help,"
said Sir Gadabout.

"Norman's asleep," said Mr Thorman. "Could you come back tomorrow?"

"Tomorrow will be too late!" called Sir Gadabout, as he rushed down the path.

But Norman wasn't asleep. How could he sleep, knowing there was an ancient Egyptian mummy looking for him? He sat on the edge of his bed and stared longingly at his chemistry set on top of the wardrobe.

"A good experiment would take my mind off things," he sighed.

Unfortunately, the chemistry set had been out of bounds since an experiment for a miracle hair restorer went drastically wrong. But that's another story.

Just then Norman heard a noise coming from inside his wardrobe.

When he opened the door he got the shock of his life. Sitting on a pile of jumpers, eating an enormous chocolate cake, was the MUMMY!

"Norman," he beamed. "I've been looking everywhere for you. Great sarcophagus you've got here."

"It's not a sarcophagus," replied Norman, his heart pounding in his chest. "It's a wardrobe!"

"It's really comfy," said the mummy, bouncing up and down on the soft pile. "I haven't got a mirror on mine."

"I don't believe it!" gasped Norman. "What are you doing in my wardrobe?"

"I'm having a snack," replied the mummy, taking a huge bite of cake. "I found it in the kitchen."

"That's my cake," frowned Norman.

"Well, you've got my egg," replied the mummy.

"But I haven't got your egg," said Norman. "It went back to the museum."

"Frolicking pharaohs!" exclaimed the mummy. "I've been hunting all over town for that egg. I even came to visit you in hospital but you were asleep."

"I thought I was dreaming," said Norman.

"The nurse thought I was a patient," said the mummy. "She made me get into bed and tucked me in so tight I could hardly get out again."

"Everyone's looking for you," said Norman. "You've even got your picture in the paper."

"Really!" smiled the mummy. "I hope they got my good side!"

Norman laughed. "I suppose you'll be going back to the museum, now that you know your egg's there," he asked.

"There's no rush," replied the mummy. "I thought I'd spend a few days here with you."

"Here?" gasped Norman. "You can't stay here!"

"Why not?" asked the mummy.

"Because the police think you've been stolen from the museum and if they find you here I'll get the blame."

"Don't worry," said the mummy. "I'll tell everyone that you didn't steal me and that *I* ate the cake."

"You can't do that!" said Norman. "Nobody must find out you're really alive."

"Why not?" asked the mummy.

73

"Because you'd get hundreds of newspaper reporters and TV cameramen following you wherever you go."

"Great!" smiled the mummy. "I'll be famous."

"It wouldn't be great, said Norman. "You'd never get any peace, and scientists would want to experiment on you."

"Oooh, I don't like the sound of that," frowned the mummy.

"I think the safest place for you is back home in your sarcophagus," said Norman.

"You're right," nodded the mummy. "This stormy weather is ruining my complexion. Soggy bandages don't suit me at all."

"You'd better hurry," said Norman. "I heard Sir Gadabout tell my dad that they're taking the whole exhibition back to Egypt tomorrow."

"Oh well," smiled the mummy. "It's been fun. I hope the next time I get out I'll be somewhere hot and sunny with not too many people."

"Are you coming back then?" asked Norman.

"As long as someone finds the egg and sneezes the magic sneeze," replied the mummy.

"So *that's* it," said Norman. "I wondered why the egg was so important to you."

Norman helped the mummy out of the wardrobe. "You're covered in chocolate cake," he gasped.

"Don't worry about that," said the mummy. "After a few thousand years of dirt, a little chocolate cake isn't going to make much difference."

They both giggled so loudly that Mr Thorman called out, "Turn off

that radio, Norman. You're supposed to be asleep."

"We'll have to get you back to the museum without being seen," said Norman. "I've got a plan. Wait here."

Norman crept downstairs and returned a few minutes later with a bundle of his dad's old clothes that were about to be given to a jumble sale.

"Put these on," he said, handing the mummy a bright yellow T-shirt with "PEDRO'S BAR TORREMOLINOS" emblazoned on the chest in large letters. Also a pair of dazzling check golfing trousers that used to give everyone a headache, an old straw hat and a pair of once fashionable sun-glasses.

"They look great," smiled the
mummy, admiring himself in the
wardrobe mirror.

Norman quietly opened his
bedroom window. "I hope you can
climb down drainpipes," he said.

Chapter Four

When Norman and the mummy got to the museum the exhibition was already being loaded into the back of a very large lorry. They could see the sarcophagus inside.

"If you get into it now," said Norman, "you won't be discovered until you get back to Egypt."

Norman gave a final wave as he watched the mummy disappear into the lorry.

The next morning at breakfast

Norman sneezed so hard he blasted his cornflakes all over the kitchen!

"Excuse me!" he apologised.

"Norman!" exclaimed his parents. "You're speaking English!"

"So I am," said Norman, and he wrote the word "cornflakes" just to check he was completely back to normal.

Two days later Mr Thorman was still laughing at his own bad mummy jokes. Throwing cushions at him didn't stop him, but something on the television *News* did!

"This is Roger Roving reporting for Channel Four News live from Egypt. The ancient Egyptian mummy that went missing from the Relic Museum in England has miraculously reappeared in its sarcophagus back in Egypt. I have with me now Sir Gadabout Binthere-Dunnit, the organiser of the exhibition, who is said to be completely baffled."

"I'm completely baffled," said Sir Gadabout. "It certainly wasn't in there when we left England."

"The Egyptian government is said to be delighted at the mummy's return, but they will not be keeping its newly acquired travelling clothes. The mystery remains; but wherever he's been, it looks like he's had a jolly good time!"

Norman will never forget the expression on his dad's face as the camera zoomed in for a close-up of the mummy.

"I . . . I . . . don't believe it,"
gasped Mr Thorman, pointing at the
screen. "How on earth? . . . They
can't be . . . I recognise that T-shirt
. . . And those trousers . . . The
thing's wearing my clothes!"

Norman ran up to his bedroom
and had the last and longest laugh.

Also in Young Puffin

The Magic Finger

Roald Dahl

**Have you ever heard of a girl with a
magic finger?**

The little girl in this story is very
unusual. When someone makes her angry
– and when she just can't stop herself –
she flashes a punishment on them with a
magic flashing finger! The results are
fantastic, magical and very funny.

Also in Young Puffin

THE LITTLE EXPLORER

Margaret Joy

Join Stanley on his thrilling voyage!

The little explorer is setting out on a long journey. He is going in search of the pinkafrillia, the rarest flower in the world. Together with Knots, the sailor, and Peckish, the parrot, Stanley travels through the jungle of Allegria. And what adventures they all have!

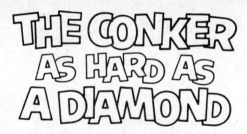

THE CONKER AS HARD AS A DIAMOND

Chris Powling

**"You were *useless*. We only had
to breathe on your conker and it
fell to bits."**

As if he could forget! Last conker season
Little Alpesh had lost every single game!
That's why he's determined this year's
going to be different. This year he's going
to win, and he won't stop until he's
Conker Champion of the Universe! The
trouble is, only a conker as hard as a
diamond will make it possible – and
where on earth is he going to find one?